Scaredy Bee

GROSSET & DUNLAP
Published by the Penguin Group
Penguin Group (USA) LLC, 375 Hudson Street, New York, New York 10014, USA

USA | Canada | UK | Ireland | Australia | New Zealand | India | South Africa | China

penguin.com
A Penguin Random House Company

ISBN 978-0-448-48691-8   10 9 8 7 6 5 4 3 2 1

"Hurry up, Barnabee!" Buzzbee called as he flew into the meadow. "We've got to get our tents up before dark."

Buzzbee started to unpack his tent while Barnabee unrolled his sleeping bag.

"Hey there, campers!" Pappa Bee called. "That looks like a good spot for your tent. I'll put mine just over there."

"Hello!" Mamma Bee sang out as she flew in, carrying Babee and a picnic blanket. Rubee and Debee followed closely behind.

"I wish we could go camping, too," Rubee complained.

"We'll go camping next week, Rubee," Mamma Bee replied. "Today we are just going to have a picnic with the boys."

"I'd rather stay in the hive," Debee said. "It's probably really *spooky* out here in the dark!"

Barnabee looked around him and trembled. He was feeling scared already.

"Come on, boys," Pappa Bee urged. "Let's get these tents up!"

Buzzbee and Barnabee fitted poles together.

Pappa Bee fumbled under the canvas.

Buzzbee wiggled the door flaps.

Finally, the tents were pitched!

The meadow slowly turned darker and darker, until finally Mamma Bee said it was time to take the girls home.

"Night-night, boys. Sleep tight," Debee called.

"I hope the spookies don't bite!" Rubee teased.

"Don't be silly, Rubee," Mamma Bee scolded.

"S-s-spookies?" Barnabee asked quietly, with a tremble in his voice. But no one heard him.

"See you in the morning!" Pappa Bee called, waving good-bye to the girls. "All right, boys, it's time for me to go to bed. Good night."

"Night-night, Pappa!" Buzzbee called.

"Night," Barnabee said.

Buzzbee and Barnabee buzzed into their tent and snuggled into their sleeping bags.

"Isn't this great, Barnabee?" asked Buzzbee. "I love camping!"

"It's a bit . . . spooky . . . ," Barnabee replied. "Oh!" he gasped. "What was that noise?"

"It was just an owl,"
Buzzbee reassured him.
"Nothing to be scared of."

"Okay, if you say so,"
Barnabee said softly.

Buzzbee had an idea.

"What was that?" Buzzbee asked, looking worried.

"What?" Barnabee replied.

"It was probably nothing," Buzzbee said, smiling. "Teddy Bee and I will go outside and check."

Outside the tent, Buzzbee waved his flashlight back and forth.

"Hello?" he called. "Any spookies out here?" He saw only Worm and Owl. "Silly old Barnabee," he said to Teddy Bee. "There's nothing to be afraid of."

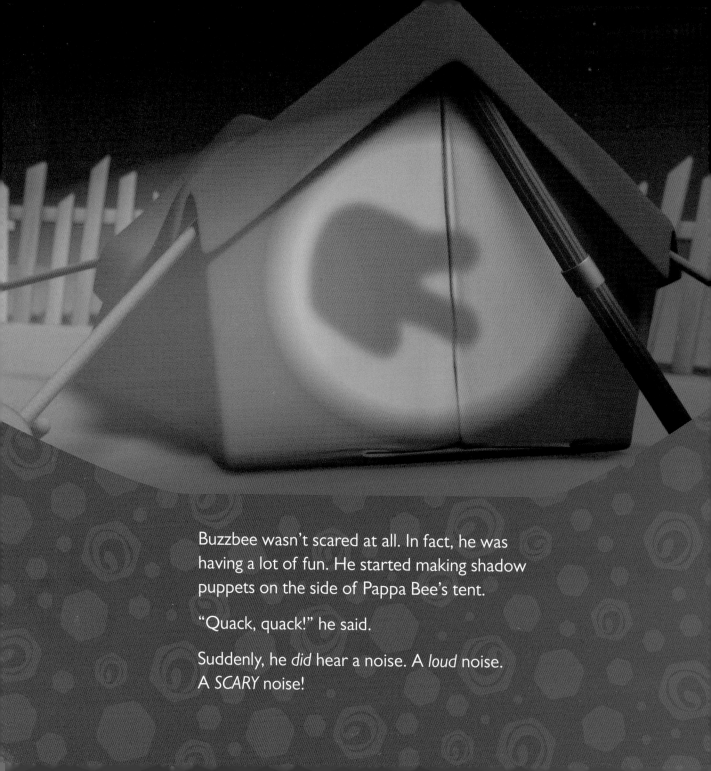

Buzzbee wasn't scared at all. In fact, he was having a lot of fun. He started making shadow puppets on the side of Pappa Bee's tent.

"Quack, quack!" he said.

Suddenly, he *did* hear a noise. A *loud* noise. A *SCARY* noise!

Suh...Snuuuh...snore!

Buzzbee gulped. For a moment it was quiet, then he heard the noise again. This time it was louder. He zoomed back into the tent.

"Barnabee!" Buzzbee yelled, shaking his friend. "Wake up, Barnabee!"

Barnabee yawned. "What's the matter, Buzzbee?" he mumbled.

"I heard a noise!" hissed Buzzbee.

"It's just an owl, like you told me," Barnabee replied sleepily.

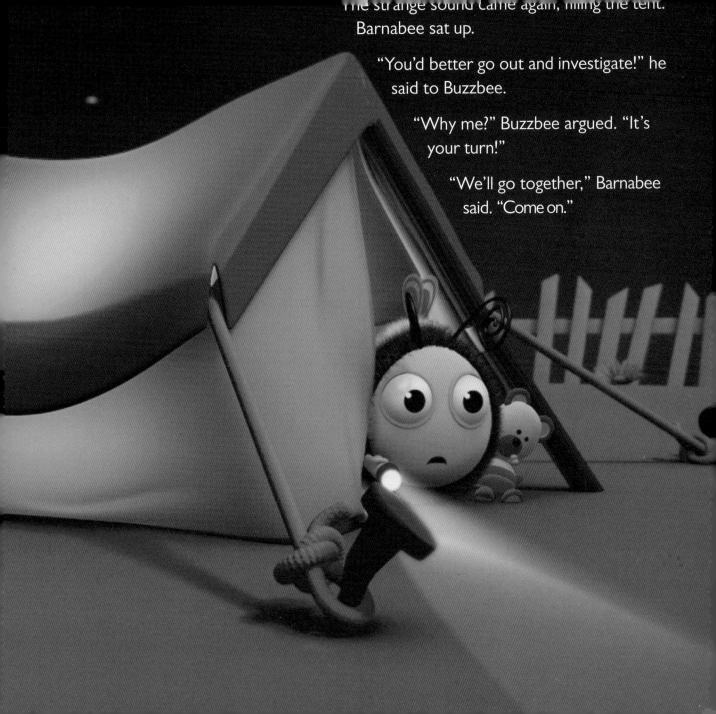

The strange sound came again, filling the tent. Barnabee sat up.

"You'd better go out and investigate!" he said to Buzzbee.

"Why me?" Buzzbee argued. "It's your turn!"

"We'll go together," Barnabee said. "Come on."

The boys tiptoed out of
their tent, Buzzbee clutching
Teddy Bee in one hand and the
flashlight in the other. They heard
the noise again and jumped up in the
air.

"What is that?" Barnabee asked.

"You said there was nothing to be scared of, Buzzbee," Barnabee said. "And now you're even more scared than I am!"

"I'm not!"

"You are!"

suh...shuuuh...snore!

"What's all that noise?" Pappa Bee called, walking out of his tent.

"Pappa?" Buzzbee asked.

"Oh!" Barnabee said, laughing. "It wasn't a wild animal. It was your papa snoring!"

"Me? Snoring?" Pappa Bee asked. "Impossible! I've never snored in my life."

Buzzbee turned to Barnabee. "I'm sorry I scared you," he said.
"I know what it's like now."

"Everybody gets scared sometimes," Pappa Bee
told them, "even when there's nothing to be
scared of."

The boys nodded. "I think
it's time for bed now,"
Buzzbee said.

Buzzbee and Barnabee buzzed back to their tent. Pappa Bee buzzed back to his, smiling.

Back in their cozy sleeping bags, the boys weren't scared anymore.

"I like camping," said Barnabee.

"So do I, Barnabee." Buzzbee yawned. "Night-night."

"Night-night, Buzzbee," replied Barnabee.

"Night-night, Owl," they both called softly before drifting off to sleep.